singing time!

grade 3

Step by step instructions for
ABRSM and other singing exams

David Turnbull

© Copyright 2002 by Bosworth & Co. Limited, London

BOSWORTH   14-15 Berners Street, London W1T 3LJ

Other series by David Turnbull include:

Singing Time!
Grades 1 and 2, uniform with this volume.

Aural Time!
Practice for ABRSM and other examinations. Separate teachers books for Grades 1 8. Pupils books available for Grades 4 with 5, 6, 7 and 8. CDs for Grades 6 and 7.

Theory Time!
Step-by-step instruction for ABRSM Theory and other examinations. Grades 1 5.

Scale Time!
Step-by-step instruction for ABRSM Piano scales, arpeggios and broken chords. Grades 1 6. Separate books for each grade.

Bosworth
14-15 Berners Street, London W1T 3LJ, UK.
Exclusive distributors:
Music Sales Limited, Newmarket Road, Bury St Edmunds, Suffolk IP33 3YB, UK.

Singing Time! Grade 3

To the Pupil

Almost everyone can sing. Singing brings pleasure to the singer – and often to the listener! It is perhaps the best way to learn about music. Your health will improve, too, because singing involves good breathing and muscle control. You don't have to buy a voice – you have one built in.

This book will help you to make the most of your natural singing gift. The songs in it provide you with a collection of music on which you can build.

Good singers don't just learn songs by ear. They must also learn how to sing at sight, so that they can learn new music quickly, and join singing groups. To do this, singers must understand the way music is written down. Knowing about rhythm, pitch, keys and intervals is just as important to singers as it is to instrumentalists.

You can learn a lot about singing from books like this, but you will learn much more if you also have a good teacher, and listen to experienced singers.

On page 47 there is a list of Italian terms used in music. More details about music theory can be found in *Theory Time!* Grade 3. Practice for aural tests can be found in *Aural Time!* Grade 3. These books, by the same author, are all published by Bosworth/Music Sales.

To the Teacher

This book contains enough material for Grade 3 ABRSM Singing (2001–2002 syllabus). Much of the material may also be used for the Initial Grade of the ABRSM Choral Singing syllabus, and teachers may also consider making use of this examination for groups of their singing pupils. Some introductory material is included in Part 6.

Examination regulations provide that *any* printed edition of a song is acceptable, and that songs may be transposed to any key to suit the voice of the performer.

Grade examinations include singing at sight, and this important aspect of a singer's equipment is stressed. The necessary theoretical background found in *Singing Time!* Grades 1 and 2 is extended in this book. Songs are grouped by key, as without a knowledge of scales and keys no skill in sight singing can be achieved.

In Grade 3 examinations, **one** song must be chosen from **each** of the lists A, B and C. In addition, one traditional song must be offered, of the candidate's own choice. **Total performance time must not exceed six minutes.** Candidates must give the examiner a list of their songs at the beginning of the examination. All songs must be sung **from memory**.

List A songs included in this book are: *Pretty Polly Oliver*, *Afton Water*, *The Ash Grove* and *The Bay of Biscay*. **List B** songs are *God Be In My Head*, *Gruss* and *Heidenröslein*. **List C** songs are *The Bare Necessities* and *The Owls*.

All other songs are traditional, any one of which may be offered in the traditional song section of the examination. Chord indications are included to help *in practice only*.

Further help with theory can be found in the author's books in the *Theory Time!* series, and with aural tests in the author's *Aural Time!* Grade 3. All these books are published by Bosworth.

David Turnbull

Part 1

Warming up

Start every practice with these exercises.

1 Breath control
Breathe at the end of every bar. Sing to four, then six, then eight.

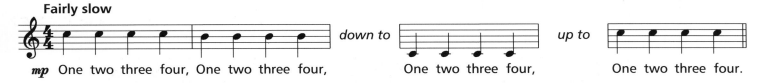

2 Vowel practice

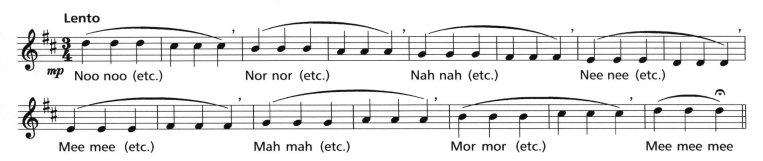

3 Control of dynamics

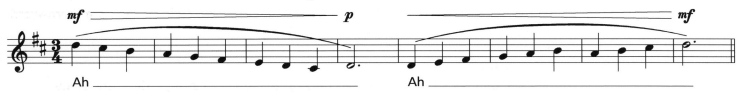

4 Arpeggios, to extend range

5 Diction
Sing slowly at first, then faster. Use lips, teeth and tongue for clear consonants.

Words by Gilbert, music by Sullivan

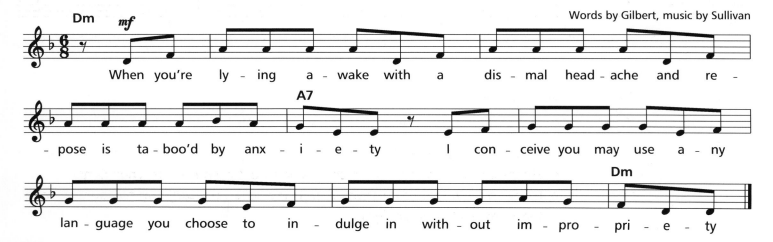

Some revision

Keys and key signatures

Make sure you know in which key a song is written.

Revise the major key signatures explained in *Singing Time!* Grades 1 and 2:

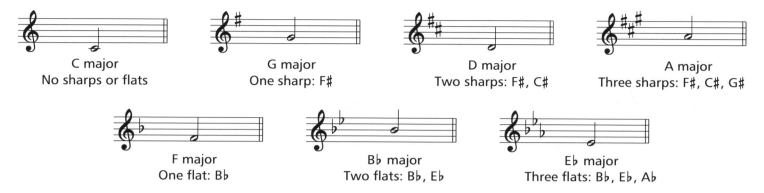

C major
No sharps or flats

G major
One sharp: F♯

D major
Two sharps: F♯, C♯

A major
Three sharps: F♯, C♯, G♯

F major
One flat: B♭

B♭ major
Two flats: B♭, E♭

E♭ major
Three flats: B♭, E♭, A♭

New keys are explained later in this book.

Words

Read over, aloud, the words of songs.

Rhythm

Clap the rhythm of the words, counting as you clap. Do this slowly at first.

Intervals

Look carefully at the intervals between the notes. For example, the first three notes of the song by Sullivan on the opposite page are each a third apart. The note A is repeated four times. Between '-wake' and 'with' there is a downward jump of a fifth, and so on.

Memorising intervals

Many people do this by remembering the starts of songs. Here are some suggestions, but make your own collection, and write them down on the music paper on page 48.

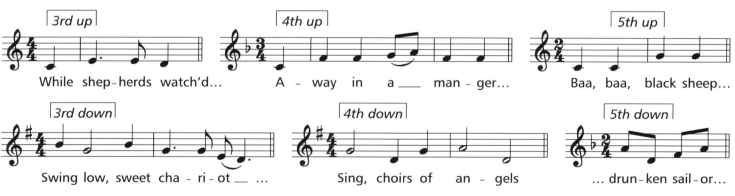

3rd up
While shep-herds watch'd...

4th up
A - way in a ___ man - ger...

5th up
Baa, baa, black sheep...

3rd down
Swing low, sweet cha - ri - ot ___ ...

4th down
Sing, choirs of an - gels

5th down
... drun - ken sail - or...

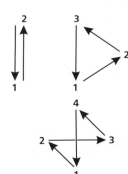

Beating Time

Practise the patterns for beating two, three and four beats to the bar.

- Two-time is 'down-up'.
- Three-time is a triangle, with the second beat going out to your right.
- Four-time is beaten as a square, with the second beat going to your left, and the third beat to your right.

Part 2

Songs in C major

C major has no sharps or flats. Here are two traditional songs in C major.
Kum Ba Ya is perhaps the way Africans pronounced 'Come by here', which they
heard said by missionaries. Sing the song slowly, and with as much expression
as possible.

Kum Ba Ya

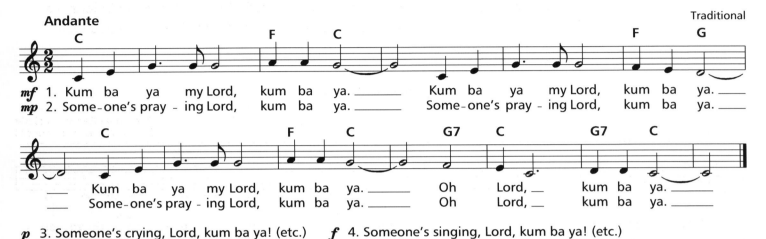

p 3. Someone's crying, Lord, kum ba ya! (etc.)   *f* 4. Someone's singing, Lord, kum ba ya! (etc.)

The Boatman's Song is mostly quick and rhythmic, but slow down at the *più
lento* markings, returning to the original pulse where *a tempo* is written.

The Boatman's Song

Melodies which change key

Most traditional songs in *Singing Time!* Grades 1 and 2 are in the same key throughout. However, many melodies change key during their course, though they almost always return to their starting key. Changing from one key to another is called **modulation**. The commonest type of modulation from a major key is to the key five notes higher – for example, from C major to G major. (See also *Theory Time!* Grade 3, p. 22.)

O Worship the Lord starts and ends in C major. It modulates to G major by introducing F♯s, returns to C major, modulates to F major by introducing B♭, then returns to C major. To appreciate the full effect of the modulations, you will need to listen to the hymn with its chords. When singing, be especially careful to get any sharps or flats absolutely in tune.

O Worship the Lord

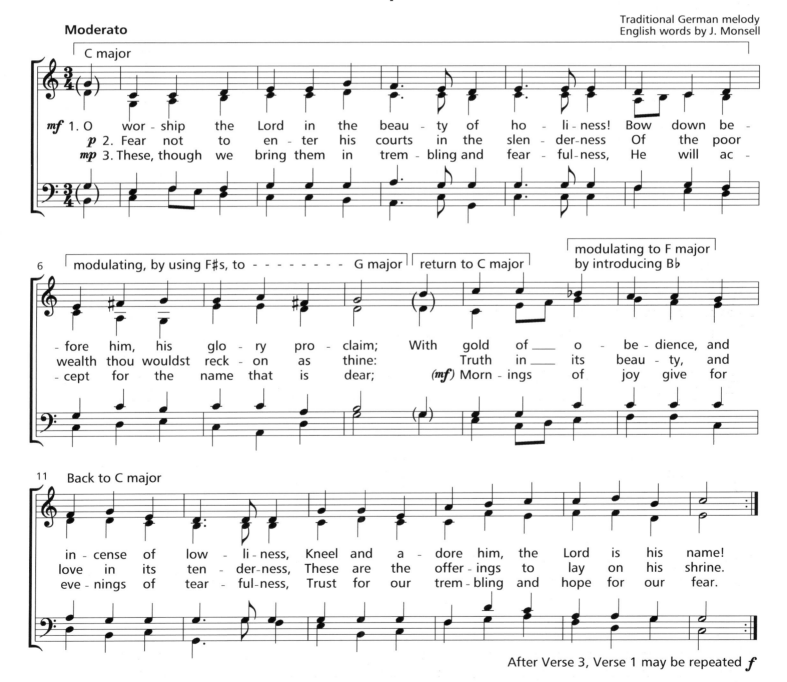

After Verse 3, Verse 1 may be repeated *f*

You may choose to sing this melody, unaccompanied, as a traditional song.

*see trees, grass
hear black bird bells echo
Fountain

taste freshwater
feel sunshine
smell freshness, grass/heather

wood - calm
serene*

Change into other book

Part 3

Songs in major keys using sharps

G major has one sharp, F♯. Here is *The Ash Grove* in G major. Notice that the melody modulates to D major in bars 25–26.

The Ash Grove

Welsh traditional
English words by Thomas Oliphant

1. Down yon-der green val-ley where stream-lets _ me - *wand*
2. Still glows the bright sun-shine o'er val - ley _ and _

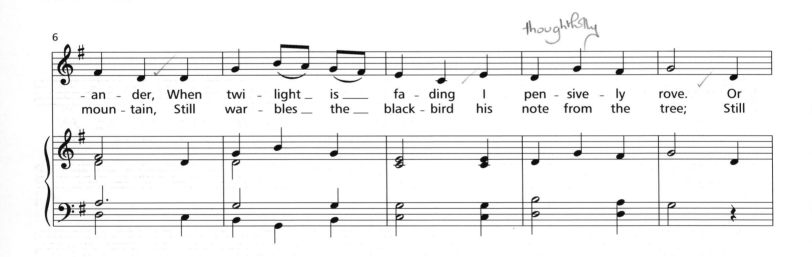

thoughtfully

-an - der, When twi - light _ is ___ fa - ding I pen - sive - ly rove. Or
moun - tain, Still war - bles _ the _ black - bird his note from the tree; Still

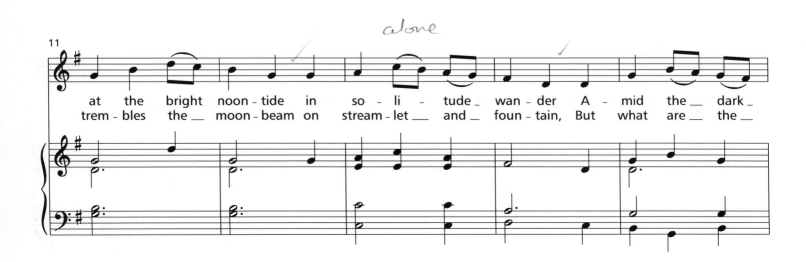

alone

at the bright noon - tide in so - li - tude _ wan - der A - mid the _ dark _
trem - bles the _ moon - beam on stream - let _ and _ foun - tain, But what are _ the _

8

Chromatic Notes

The second note of *Down By The Riverside* is A♯, which is not a note in G major. When a note outside the key is used, the note is called a **chromatic note**. Such notes add colour to a phrase, but make sure they are in tune.

The song is **syncopated**, which means that some notes are sung 'off the beat'. You will find it helpful to beat time for yourself as you sing. If you don't understand the Italian direction at the beginning of the piece, look it up on page 47.

1st beat   2nd beat   1st beat   2nd beat

lay down   my   sword and shield _____

Down by the Riverside

Songs in D major

D major has two sharps – F♯ and C♯. *Gruss* ('Greeting') was originally written to German words. An English translation is printed underneath the German words. Sing in either language. If you have someone who can teach you the pronunciation, try singing the song in German. Read the English too, even if you decide to sing in German, as a general understanding of the meaning is essential.

The words of *The Blue Bells of Scotland* are a dialogue. One person asks questions, the other answers. Get contrast between the two, by altering dynamics and tone quality.

The Blue Bells of Scotland

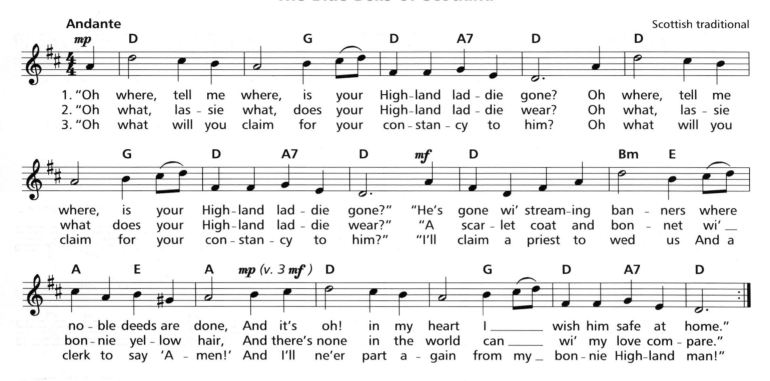

1. "Oh where, tell me where, is your High-land lad-die gone? Oh where, tell me
2. "Oh what, las-sie what, does your High-land lad-die wear? Oh what, las-sie
3. "Oh what will you claim for your con-stan-cy to him? Oh what will you

where, is your High-land lad-die gone?" "He's gone wi' stream-ing ban-ners where
what does your High-land lad-die wear?" "A scar-let coat and bon-net wi'___
claim for your con-stan-cy to him?" "I'll claim a priest to wed us And a

no-ble deeds are done, And it's oh! in my heart I_____ wish him safe at home."
bon-nie yel-low hair, And there's none in the world can____ wi' my love com-pare."
clerk to say 'A-men!' And I'll ne'er part a-gain from my_ bon-nie High-land man!"

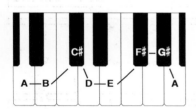

Songs in A major

A major has three sharps – F♯, C♯ and G♯. Remember that ⁶⁄₈ time is compound duple time, with two dotted crotchet beats to the bar. Sing this song with a good swing.

The Lincolnshire Poacher

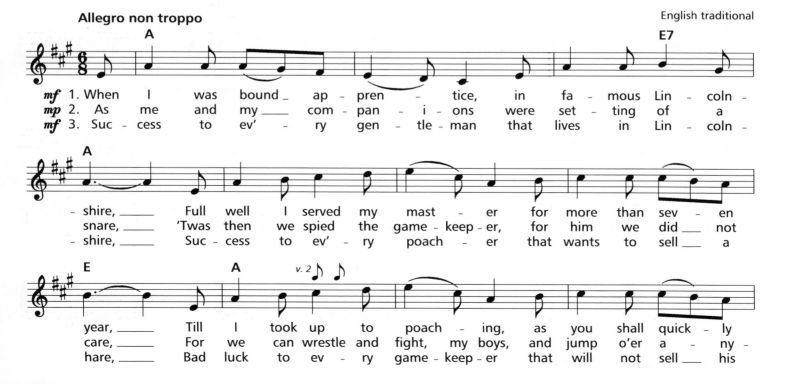

1. When I was bound_ ap-pren-tice, in fa-mous Lin-coln-
2. As me and my___ com-pan-i-ons were set-ting of a
3. Suc-cess to ev'-ry gen-tle-man that lives in Lin-coln-

- shire,_____ Full well I served my mast-er for more than sev-en
snare,_____ 'Twas then we spied the game-keep-er, for him we did__ not
- shire,_____ Suc-cess to ev'-ry poach-er that wants to sell__ a

year,_____ Till I took up to poach-ing, as you shall quick-ly
care,_____ For we can wrestle and fight, my boys, and jump o'er a-ny-
hare,_____ Bad luck to ev-'ry game-keep-er that will not sell__ his

hear;
-where; } Oh! 'tis my de-light on a shi-ning night in the sea-son of the
deer;

year. Oh 'tis my de-light on a shi-ning night in the sea-son of the year. ___

God Be In My Head is written for a four-part choir. Sing the melody line only,
with a wide range of dynamics and a very soft ending.

God Be In My Head

H. Walford Davies

(Piano only)   God be in my head, And in my un-der-

-stand-ing; God be in my eyes, And in my look-ing; God be in my

mouth, And in my speak-ing; God be in my heart, And in my

think-ing; God be at mine end, And at my de-part-ing.

Songs in E major

E major has four sharps – F♯, C♯, G♯ and D♯.

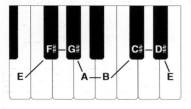

Key signature

Scale of E major   Arpeggio of E major

Afton Water

Scottish traditional melody
Words by Robert Burns

Gently, but with movement

Voice

Piano

p 1. Flow gen - tly, sweet Af - ton, a -
mp 2. Thou stock - dove whose ec - ho re -

- mong thy green _ braes, _ Flow gen - tly, I'll _ sing _ thee a _
- sounds thro' the _ glen, _ Ye wild, whist - ling _ black - birds in _

song in _ thy _ praise; My _ Ma - ry's a - sleep by thy
yon thorn - y _ den, Thou _ green - crest - ed _ lap - wing, thy

14

The Minstrel Boy

Old Irish melody
Words by Thomas Moore

1. The Min-strel Boy to the war is gone, In the ranks of death you'll find him; His
2. The Min-strel fell! But the foe-man's chain Could not bring that proud soul un-der; The

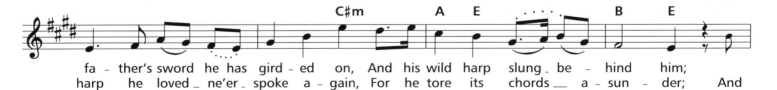

fa - ther's sword he has gird-ed on, And his wild harp slung be-hind him;
harp he loved ne'er spoke a-gain, For he tore its chords a-sun-der; And

"Land of song!" said the war-rior bard, "Tho' all the world be-trays thee, One
said "No chains shall sul-ly thee, Thou soul of love and brav'-ry! Thy

sword, at least, thy rights shall guard, One faith-ful harp shall praise thee!"
songs were made for the pure and free, They shall nev-er sound in slav'-ry!"

Heidenröslein

Franz Schubert
Words by Goethe, translated by Natalia Macfarren

1. Saw a boy a morn-ing rose Bloom-ing in the hea - ther,
2. Said the boy I'll cut you now, Rose a-mong the hea - ther,
3. But the boy im-pa-tient cull'd Rose a-mong the hea - ther,

As her dain-ty leaves un-close, Straight to gaze on her he goes,
Said the rose: My thorn I vow, You will feel it's sharp-en'd now,
Rose prick'd sharp-ly as he pull'd, But her days a-las were told,

In the sum-mer wea - ther. Rose, Oh pret-ty rose so red,
Me you shall not ga - ther. }
Wound-ed both to geth - er. }

Rose a-mong the hea - ther.

You may prefer to sing *Heidenröslein* in the original German. Check your pronunciation with a German speaker.

Double sharps and double flats

In bar 9 of *Heidenröslein*, notice the accidental sign ✗ in front of the first note of the syllable '-len'.

This sign shows that the note following it is a **double sharp**, and must be raised by *two* semitones. F double sharp is therefore the same note in pitch as G natural.

Double flats exist also, and the sign for them is ♭♭. This sign in front of a note means that the pitch of the note must be lowered by two semitones.

Stance and presentation

Stand as still as you can when performing songs. Keep your head up, and 'take in' the listeners in your look. Remember that in accompanied songs the piano part is important too, so stay still until the piano part ends. Look at the audience as much as you can.

If you need to use printed music when practising, hold it in both hands at a comfortable level – not too high.

Part 4

Songs in major keys using flats

F major has one flat, B♭. Notice the chromatic G♯ near the start of this song.

The Bare Necessities

Bright Tempo *(with spirit)*

Words and music by Terry Gilkyson

1.3. Look for the bare ne - ces - si - ties, the sim - ple bare ne -
2. (Look for the) bare ne - ces - si - ties, the sim - ple bare ne -

ces - si - ties; __ For - get a - bout your wor - ries and your strife.
ces - si - ties; __ For - get a - bout your wor - ries and your strife.

I mean the bare ne - ces - si - ties, __ or Moth - er Na - ture's
I mean the bare ne - ces - si - ties, __ that's why a bear can

B flat major

B flat major has two flats – B♭ and E♭.

Sing this American song.

Give Me That Old-time Religion

Chorus

Fairly fast

Traditional spiritual

You may like to clap as you sing.

Clap *either* on beats 1 and 3 of each bar, *or* on beats 2 and 4.

The Bay of Biscay

John Davy
arranged by John Farmer

1. Loud roar'd the dreadful thunder, The rain a deluge showr's, The clouds were rent asunder By lightning's vivid pow'rs. The night was drear and dark, Our poor devoted bark, Till next day there she lay In the Bay of Biscay O!

2. Now, dash'd upon the billow, Her op'ning timbers creak, Each fears a wat'ry pillow, None stop the dreadful leak. To cling to slipp'ry shrouds, Each breathless seaman crowds, As she lay till next day In the Bay of Biscay O!

E flat major

E flat major has three flats – B♭, E♭ and A♭.

Sing *Deep River* as expressively as possible.

Deep River

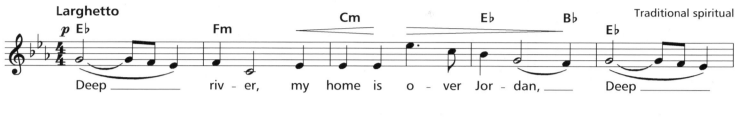

Deep _____ riv - er, my home is o - ver Jor - dan, ___ Deep _____

riv - er, Lord I want to cross o - ver in - to camp ground. O don't you want to go ___ to that

gos - pel ___ feast, ___ That prom - ised ___ land ___ where all ___ is peace? ___ O

don't you want to go ___ to that prom - ised land, that land ___ where all is peace? _____

Shenandoah

1. Oh, Shen - an - doah, ___ I long to hear you, } A - way, you roll - ing
   Shen - an - doah, ___ I love your daugh - ter.

ri - ver. Oh, Shen - an - doah, ___ I long to hear-you, } A - way, I'm bound to
          Oh, Shen - an - doah, ___ I love your daugh - ter.

go 'Cross the wide Mis - sour - i. 2. Oh, - sour - i.

3. Oh, Shenandoah, I took a notion, *Away …*
   To sail across the stormy ocean. *Away …*

4. Oh, Shenandoah, I'm bound to leave you, *Away …*
   Oh, Shenandoah, I'll not deceive you. *Away …*

This song shouldn't be sung too quickly, but it does need to be sung with a lilt.

Pretty Polly Oliver

Traditional
arr. W Chappell

Verse 4

"A maid?" said the Captain, "then throw her in jail."
"Oh, no!" pleaded Polly, who told her sad tale,
And when a great vict'ry had ended the strife,
The Captain took Polly and made her his wife.

prove, I'll list for a sol - dier and fol - low my love."
side, And as Pol - ly lift - ed him she knew __ he had died.
fraid?" "Oh Sir! I'm no sol - dier," said Pol - ly, "I'm a maid."

A flat major

A flat major has four flats – B♭, E♭, A♭ and D♭.

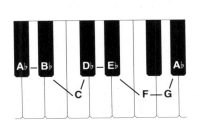

Key signature

Scale of A♭ major   Arpeggio of A♭ major

Robin Adair

Traditional Celtic melody
Words by Robert Burns

Andante

A♭   E♭   A♭

p 1. What's this dull town to me? Rob - in's __ not __ near; What was't I
mp 2. What made th'as - sem - bly shine? Rob - in __ A - dair; What made the
p 3. But now thou'rt far from me, Rob - in __ A - dair. And now thou'rt

E♭   A♭   E♭   A♭

wish'd to see, What wish'd to __ hear? Where's all the joy and mirth Made this town
ball so fine? Rob - in __ was __ there. What, when the play was o'er, What made my
cold to me, Rob - in __ A - dair. Yet he I lov'd so well, Still in my

E♭   E♭7   A♭

heav'n on earth? Oh! they're all __ fled with thee, Rob - in __ A - dair.
heart so sore? Oh! it __ was __ part - ing with Rob - in __ A - dair.
heart shall dwell. Oh! I __ can __ ne'er for - get Rob - in __ A - dair.

25

Part 5

Beyond major keys

So far, songs have been in major keys. However, you will often meet songs in minor keys, or which use other types of scale-like modes. You will learn more about minor scales and modes later. Here are some songs to sing now.

E minor

E minor shares the same key signature as G major – F♯.

David of the White Rock

Welsh traditional melody
English words by John Oxenford

Slowly and sadly

mp 1. Da - vid __ the __ Bard on his bed __ of __ death lies, Pale are his fea - tures and
p 2. Give me __ my __ harp, my com - pan - ion __ so __ long, Let it once more add __ its

dim are __ his __ eyes; Yet all a - round him __ his __ glance wild - ly __
voice to __ my __ song; Though my old fin - gers __ are __ pal - sied __ and __

roves __ Till __ it a - lights on __ the harp __ that he loves.
weak, __ Still __ my __ good __ harp __ for __ its mast - er will speak.

mp 3. Often the hearts of our chiefs it has stirred,
When its loud summons to battle was heard;
Harp of my country, dear harp of the brave,
Let thy last notes hover over my grave.

G minor

G minor shares the same key signature as B flat major – B♭ and E♭.

Once I Had a Sweetheart

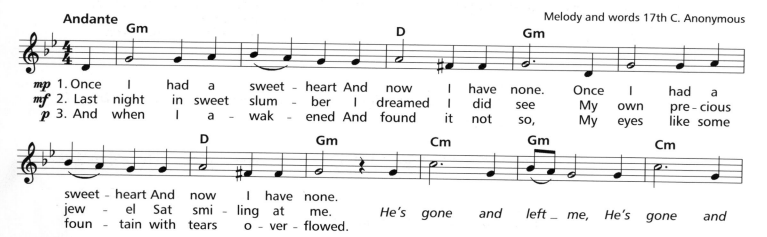

Melody and words 17th C. Anonymous

Andante

mp 1. Once I had a sweet - heart And now I have none. Once I had a
mf 2. Last night in sweet slum - ber I dreamed I did see My own pre - cious
p 3. And when I a - wak - ened And found it not so, My eyes like some

sweet - heart And now I have none.
jew - el Sat smi - ling at me. *He's gone and left __ me, He's gone and*
foun - tain with tears o - ver - flowed.

left _ me He's gone and left me to sor - row and moan. _____

4. I'll venture through England,
   Through France and to Spain;
   All my life I'll venture
   The watery main.
        He's gone and left me, etc.

C minor

C minor has the same key signature as E flat major. Note 6 can be A♭ or A♮, and note 7 can be either B♭ or B♮.

1 2 3 4 5 6 7 1' 7 6 5 4 3 2 1

Charlie is my Darling

Scottish traditional
Words by Lady Nairne

f Char - lie is m' dar - lin', m' dar - lin', m' dar - lin', Char - lie is m' dar - lin', the young Che - va - lier.

1. 'Twas on a Mon - day morn - ing Right ear - ly in the year, When
2. As he came march - ing up the street The pipes played loud and clear, And

Char - lie came to our ____ town The ___ young ___ Che - va - lier. Oh!
all the folks came run - ning out To ___ meet the Che - va - lier Oh!

D.C. for verses 2, 3 & 4

mf 3. Wi' Hieland bonnets on their heads,
       And claymores bright and clear,
       They came to fight for Scotland's right,
       And for the Chevalier.
            Oh! Charlie is m'darlin', etc.

mp 4. They've left their bonnie Hieland hills,
       Their wives and bairnies dear,
   cresc. To draw the sword for Scotland's lord,
   f   The young Chevalier.
            Oh! Charlie is m'darlin', etc.

F minor

F minor has the same key signature as A flat major. Note 6 can be D♭ or D♮, Note 7 can be E♭ or E♮.

1 2 3 4 5 6 7 1' 7 6 5 4 3 2 1

The next song, *The Owls*, is in F minor.

The Owls

Words and music by Peter Jenkyns

The melody of *When Johnny Comes Marching Home* is modal.

When Johnny Comes Marching Home

Traditional melody
Words by Patrick Gilmore

The last song in this section uses a pentatonic (five-note) scale – C, D, F, G and A.

I Gave My Love a Cherry

Traditional

Part 6

Singing with other people

Singing by yourself, or with an accompanist, is fun. But you can get even more enjoyment by singing with other people, either in small groups or in a large choir.

Rounds

Try singing this simple round. Three voices, or groups of voices, are needed. When Voice 1 reaches the end of the first line, Voice 2 starts at the beginning. When Voice 2 has reached the end of the first line, Voice 3 starts. When a voice has finished, it may start singing the round again. A leader is needed, to bring the round to an end, and to vary dynamics.

Great Tom is Cast

Moderato

White

Great   Tom is   cast,   and

Christ Church bells ring one, two, three, four, five,

six, and Tom comes last.

Here is a round for four voices.

London's Burning

Andante

Traditional

Lon - don's burn - ing, Lon - don's burn - ing,

fetch the en - gines, fetch the en - gines;

Fire! Fire!   Fire!   Fire!

Pour on wa - ter, pour on wa - ter.

The Gendarmes' Duet is for two voices or groups of singers. The vocal lines can be sung by unbroken voices at the written pitch, or by broken voices an octave lower. It comes from an operetta, so singers can use actions if they wish, and even dance during the piano interludes between the verses!

The Gendarmes' Duet
(from the opera *Geneviève de Brabant*)

Jacques Offenbach
English words by H. B. Farnie

When dan - ger looms, we're nev - er there!
Com - mune with na - ture face to face!
Pro - vi - ded that they make it right!

cha - ry,
ru - ral
qui - et

But when we
Un - to our
But if they

Or lit - tle boys that do no
Re - freshed by Na - ture's ho - ly
Or give to us our pro - per

meet a help - less wo - - man,
beat then back re - turn - - ing
do not seem to see it,

(after all verses)

harm.
charm.
terms!

We run them in,

we run them in, We show them

(after all verses)

We run them in,

we run them in,

we're the bold Gen - darmes! We run them in,

We run them in, we run them

we run them in, We show them we're the bold Gen - darmes!

in, we run them in, We show them we're the bold Gen - darmes!

Part 7

Singing at sight

Singing at sight is difficult at first. Here is an example of the type of test you might have to sing at sight:

False Lamkin

Folksong collected and arranged by Cecil Sharp

In examinations, you will be played the key chord and key note, and then given half a minute to prepare the test. You will be played the key chord and key note again, just before you have to sing the piece. When practising, though, take as much time as is necessary to master the steps listed below – you will get faster with experience.

When you sing tests in exams, you may sing notes to the printed words, *or* to any vowel, *or* to sol-fa names. When practising, though, it is better to sing the words, as they help you understand the mood of the song.

- Work out the rhythm. Clap the rhythm of the introduction, then the words.
- Decide what key the piece is in, and on which note of the key it starts. See if your starting note is played by the piano in the introduction.
- The melody will be a mixture of stepwise movement and jumps. Work out the intervals of any jumps before you start.
- Look at the dynamics and any expression marks, and be sure to include them.
- Sing the song slowly at first. When confident, sing it at its suggested tempo. In the exam, the accompaniment will be played by the examiner, who will therefore set the speed for you.

Using this approach, prepare and sing the song above, then continue with the other examples on the next pages.

Allegro ma non troppo

3.

I'd __ just as soon be a beg-gar as a king, And the

rea-son I'll tell you for why; A king can-not swag-ger nor

drink like a beg-gar, Nor be half so __ hap-py as I.

Allegro moderato

7.

Fair Ros – a – lind in woe – ful wise, Six

hearts hath bound in thrall; As yet she un – de – ter – min'd is Which

she her spouse will call, _____ Which she her spouse will call.

43

Though the melody of this example is simple, the accompaniment is quite complex.

Adagio   J. S. Bach (adapted)

8.

Be - side _ Thy cra - dle here I stand, O _ Thou that ev - er _

giv - - est. Ac - cept me; 'tis my mind _ and heart, My

soul, my strength, through ev - 'ry part That Thou from me re - quir - est.

44

No stir in the air, no stir in the sea, The

ship was still as she __ may be, _____ Her sails from hea - ven re -

- cei - ved mo - tion Her keel was stea - dy in __ the o - cean. _____

Musical terms

Tempo

a tempo	in time (*tempo* means time)
adagietto	slow, but less slow than *adagio*
adagio	slow, leisurely
allegro	fairly fast
allegretto	fairly fast, but less fast than *allegro*
andante	at a moderate walking pace
andantino	a little faster than *andante*
grave	very slow and solemn
larghetto	fairly slow
largo	slow and dignified, broad
lento	slow
moderato	at a moderate speed
presto	fast
tempo comodo	at a comfortable speed
vivace, vivo	fast and lively

Changes to Tempo

accelerando	getting faster gradually
allargando	broadening – slower
rallentando (rall.)	getting slower gradually
ritardando (rit.) (or *ritard.*)	getting slower gradually
ritenuto (rit.)	holding back
rubato tempo rubato	with some freedom in time
stringendo	gradually getting faster
tenuto (ten.)	held

Dynamics

forte (*f*)	loud
forte piano (*fp*)	loud, then immediately soft
fortissimo (*ff*)	very loud
mezzo forte (*mf*)	moderately loud
piano (*p*)	quiet
pianissimo (*pp*)	very quiet
mezzo piano (*mp*)	moderately quiet

Changes to Dynamics

crescendo (cresc.)	gradually getting louder
decrescendo	gradually getting quieter
diminuendo (dim.)	gradually getting quieter
sforzato, sforzando	accented loudly (*sf* or *sfz*)

Manner of performance

ad libitum	freely, as you wish
agitato	agitated
amore, con amore	with love
animato	animated and lively
brio, con	with vigour
cantabile	in a singing style
deciso, con deciso	with decision
delicato, con delicato	with delicacy
dolce	sweetly
energico, con	with energy
espressivo	expressively
forza, con forza	with force
giocoso	playful
grazioso	graceful
largamente	broadly
legato	smoothly
leggiero	lightly
maestoso	majestic
marcato	marked
marziale	in a martial style
mesto	sad
moto, mosso	movement
pesante	heavy
risoluto, con	with determination
ritmico	rhythmically
scherzando, scherzoso	playful, joking
semplice	simple, uncomplicated
sostenuto	sustained
staccato	sharp, detached
tranquillo	tranquil, calm
triste, tristamente	sad, sorrowful

Other

da capo (D.C.)	(repeat) from the beginning
dal segno (D.S.)	(repeat) from the sign
fine	end
prima volta	first time
seconda volta	second time

Qualifying words

Molto in front of a word means 'very' or 'much'. For example, *molto allegro* means 'very fast'.
Meno means 'less'. *Più* means 'more'. *Senza* means 'without'. *Con* means 'with'. *E* or *ed* means 'and'.
Non means 'not'. *Troppo* means 'too much'.
Poco in front of a word means 'little', or 'slightly'. For example, *poco crescendo* means 'getting slightly louder'.
Assai means 'very'. *Simile* means 'in the same way'. *Al* or *alla* means 'in the manner of'. *Ma* means 'but'.
Sempre means 'always'. *Subito* means 'immediately'. *Tanto* means 'so much'.

Index of songs

Use the staves below to write down the openings of tunes you choose to help you remember intervals (see page 5).

The author wishes to record his thanks to

Katherine Davies of Bosworth/Music Sales for expert editing;
Paul Terry of Musonix, for advice and admirable typesetting;
Diana Turnbull for German translations, and for many hours of help with text and proof-reading.